Read with Mummy

The Ugly Duckling

Story retold by Janet Brown

Illustrations by Ken Morton

Mother Duck is very excited. Her eggs are nearly ready to hatch. Soon she will be the proud mother of six little ducklings.

Her friend says, "One of your eggs is much bigger than the others."

"ALL my little ducklings will be beautiful," sniffs Mother Duck.

Secretly she is worried. But she does not want the other farmyard animals to know that.

How many little ducklings are about to be born?

It's time! Five eggs start to crack, and five fluffy ducklings wriggle out of their shells.

"Ahhh!" say all the farmyard animals.

Then the sixth egg, the BIG egg, starts to crack. And out steps a very strange bird.

"Oh!" cry the farmyard animals. Then they look at Mother Duck. She pretends not to notice that her sixth baby is a very ugly duckling indeed.

at does Mother Duck pretend not to notice about her sixth duckling?

Mother Duck and her six ducklings go for a swim. Five little ducklings splish splash together in the water. But the sixth duckling is too big to play with the others.

"Ouch!" they cry. "Go away, Ugly Duckling!" They swim away from him, laughing. The Ugly Duckling is unhappy. He decides to run away. But wherever he goes, things are always the same.

"What an ugly duckling!" cry the wild ducks.
"What a strange bird!" cry the geese.
"Go away!" they cry.
"One day," thinks the Ugly Duckling, "I will be beautiful, and then they'll be sorry." But he does not believe it.

What do the Ugly Duckling's brothers and sisters say to him?

The Ugly Duckling is strong and brave. But he is also lonely, and winter is coming. He makes himself a home by the side of a big lake. One morning he wakes up and watches a family of swans flying across the sky.

"How graceful they are!" he thinks. "How happy they must be!"

He sighs. It is getting colder.

Where does the Ugly Duckling make his new home?

Snow begins to fall. The lake freezes over. In the distance the Ugly Duckling can see a farmhouse. There are bright lights and voices.

"I wish I lived over there," he thinks to himself.

But he knows they will only laugh at him.

So he goes out onto the frozen lake instead. His big feet make wonderful skates. The Ugly Duckling skates on the ice for hours. He has fun by himself.

What does the Ugly Duckling do out on the lake by himself?

The ice melts. Spring has come! The other birds start to arrive back at the lake. The water is full of wild ducks and geese, chattering and laughing. They are glad to be together again.

The Ugly Duckling hides. He waits for someone to notice him, but everyone is busy.

Why have the other birds started to arrive back at the lake?

"I don't care," says the Ugly Duckling. He notices everyone else flying around. He stretches his wings and begins to flap. Suddenly he is up in the sky, away from the chattering voices.

"I can fly!" he cries.

The sky is very blue. Up here it is quiet. He feels the sun on his wings. The wind slips past him. It feels wonderful.

Do you recognise the Ugly Duckling in this picture?
Can you guess what has happened?

He flies past a family of swans.

"My goodness!" they say. "What a handsome bird!"

The Ugly Duckling turns around in surprise. "ME?" he asks.

"A most fine and handsome bird!" say the swans. "One of the most beautiful we have ever seen!"

The Ugly Duckling is so surprised that he crashes down into the lake. The he looks into the water to see his reflection.

A snowy white swan is looking back up at him!

What does the Ugly Duckling see reflected in the lake?

All the swans crowd around him. "He must be a prince," they say. "We would like to be his friend."

"Where do you come from?" they ask. "Why haven't we seen you before?"

The Beautiful Swan smiles. "I've been here all the time!" he says.

What is the Ugly Duckling's new name?

On a piece of paper, practise writing these words:

flying south

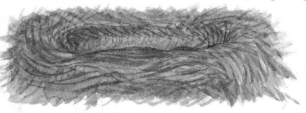

nest

eggs

swan

duckling